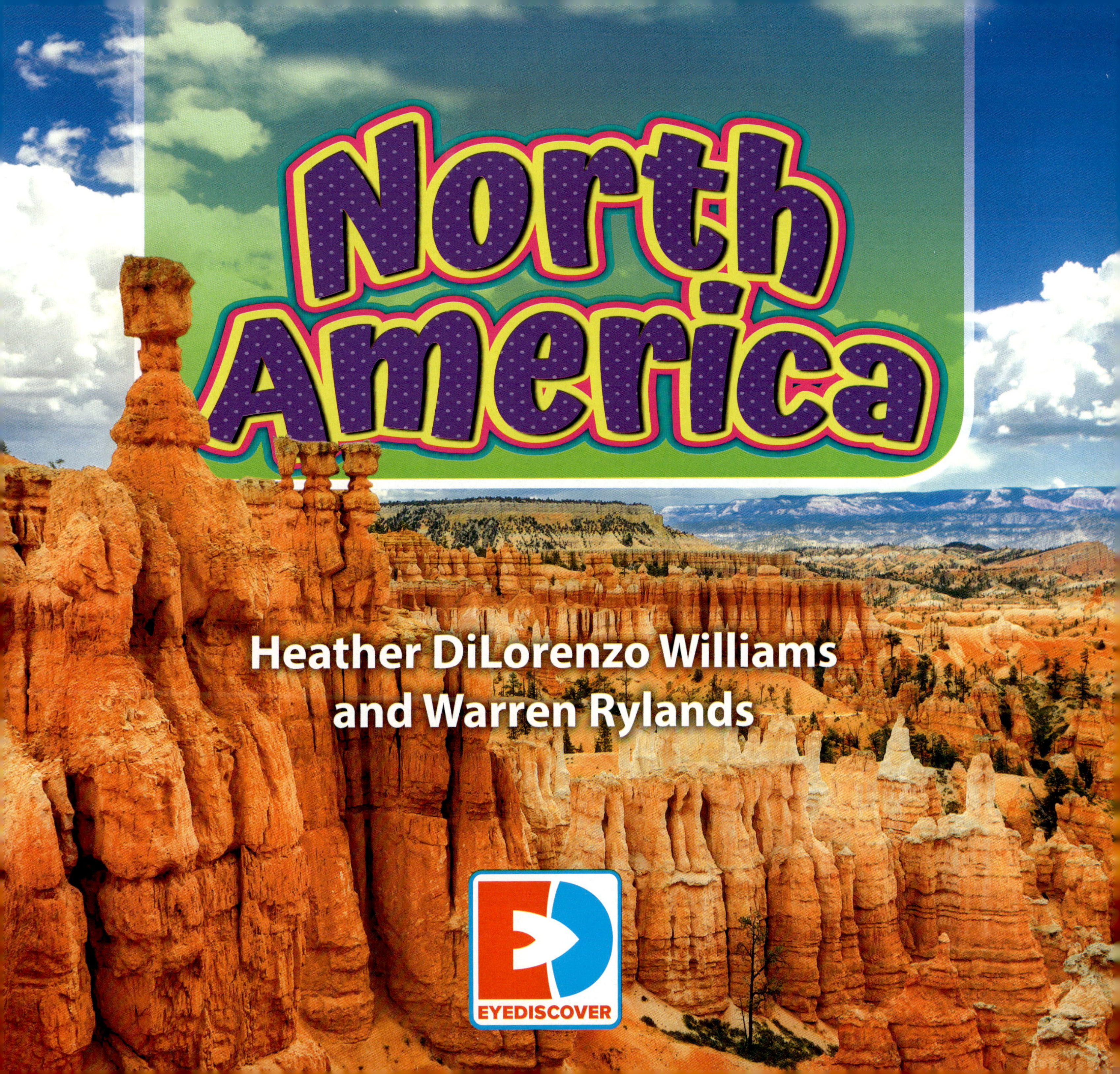
North America
Heather DiLorenzo Williams and Warren Rylands
EYEDISCOVER

Go to www.eyediscover.com and enter this book's unique code.

BOOK CODE

AVC33949

EYEDISCOVER brings you optic readalongs that support active learning.

Published by AV² by Weigl
350 5th Avenue, 59th Floor New York, NY 10118
Website: www.eyediscover.com

Library of Congress Control Number: 2018953513

ISBN 978-1-4896-8325-0 (hardcover)

Printed in the United States of America
in Brainerd, Minnesota
1 2 3 4 5 6 7 8 9 0 22 21 20 19 18

082018
120917

Project Coordinator: John Willis
Designer: Mandy Christiansen

Weigl acknowledges Alamy and Shutterstock as the primary image suppliers for this title.

EYEDISCOVER provides enriched content, optimized for tablet use, that supplements and complements this book. EYEDISCOVER books strive to create inspired learning and engage young minds in a total learning experience.

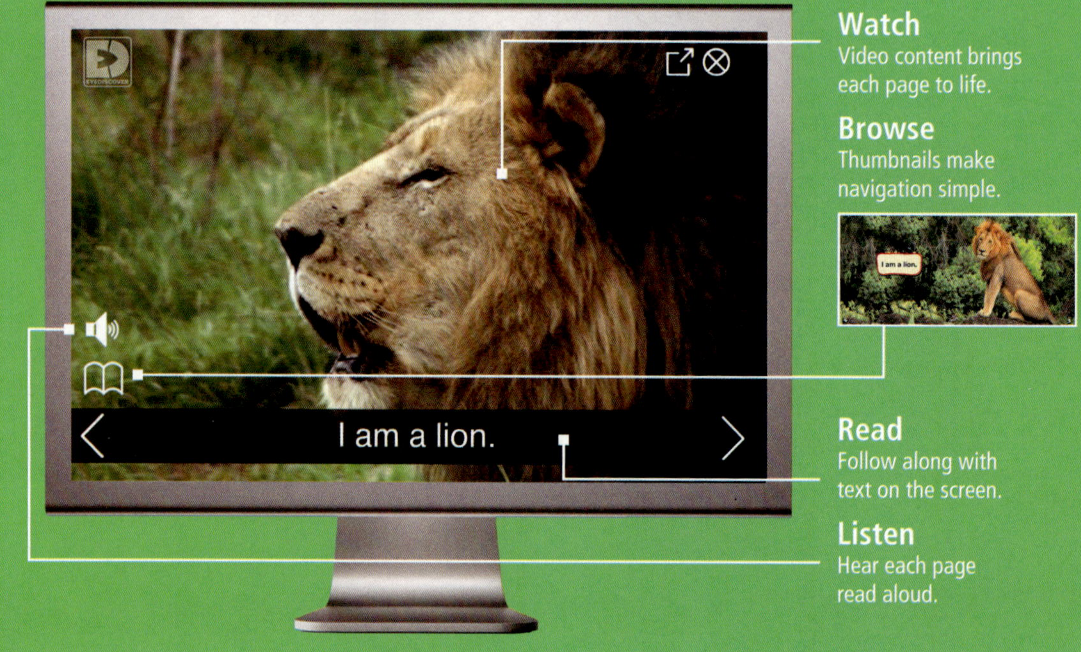

Your EYEDISCOVER Optic Readalongs come alive with...

Audio
Listen to the entire book read aloud.

Video
High resolution videos turn each spread into an optic readalong.

OPTIMIZED FOR

- ✓ TABLETS
- ✓ WHITEBOARDS
- ✓ COMPUTERS
- ✓ AND MUCH MORE!

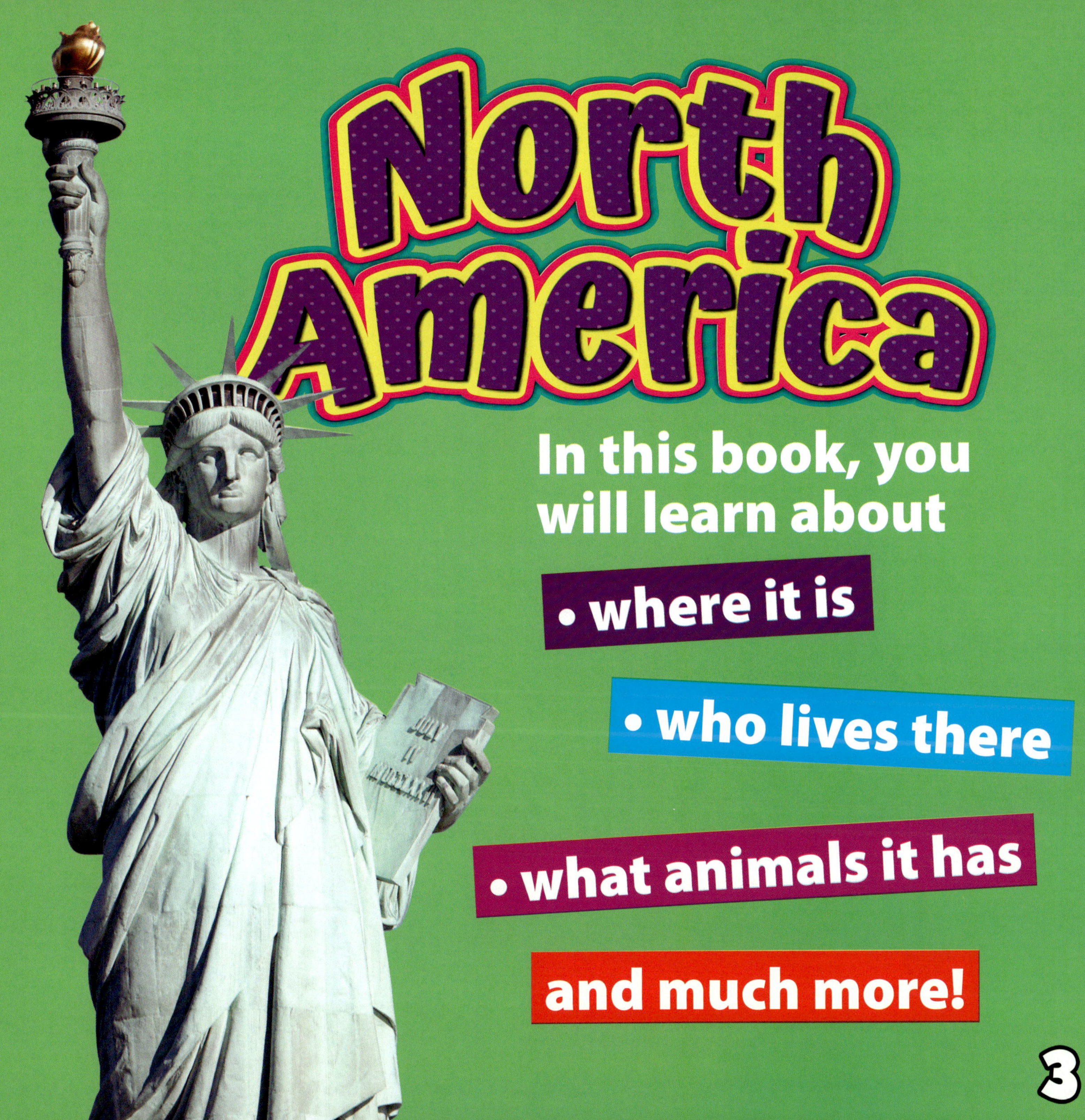

North America

In this book, you will learn about

- where it is
- who lives there
- what animals it has

and much more!

North America is the third-largest continent on Earth.

There are 23 different countries in North America. The United States and Canada take up the most space.

Mexico City is the biggest city in North America. About 8.9 million people live there.

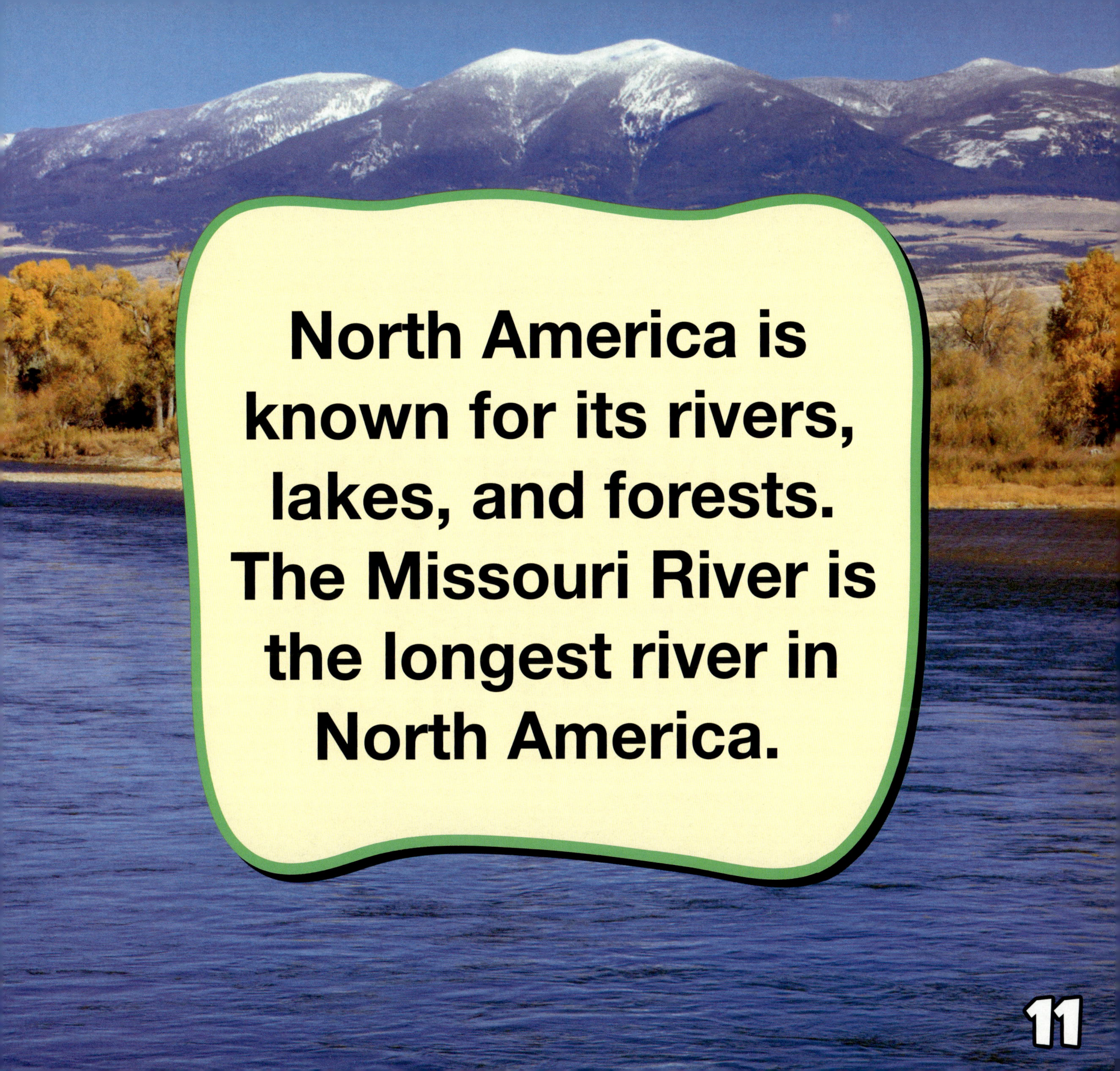

North America is known for its rivers, lakes, and forests. The Missouri River is the longest river in North America.

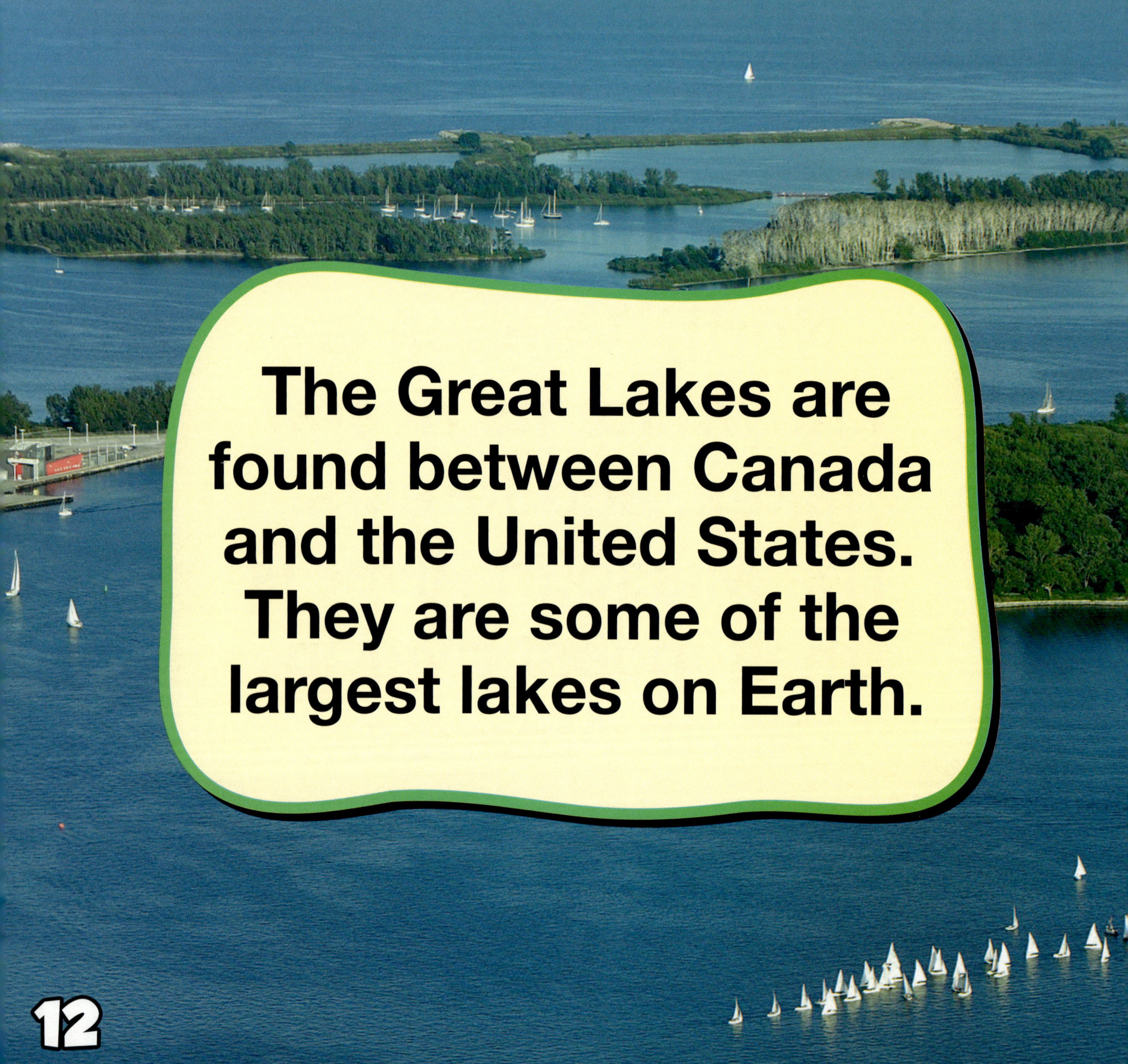

The Great Lakes are found between Canada and the United States. They are some of the largest lakes on Earth.

Many different plants and animals live in North America. The bison is the largest land animal in North America.

The California redwoods are the largest and tallest trees in the world.

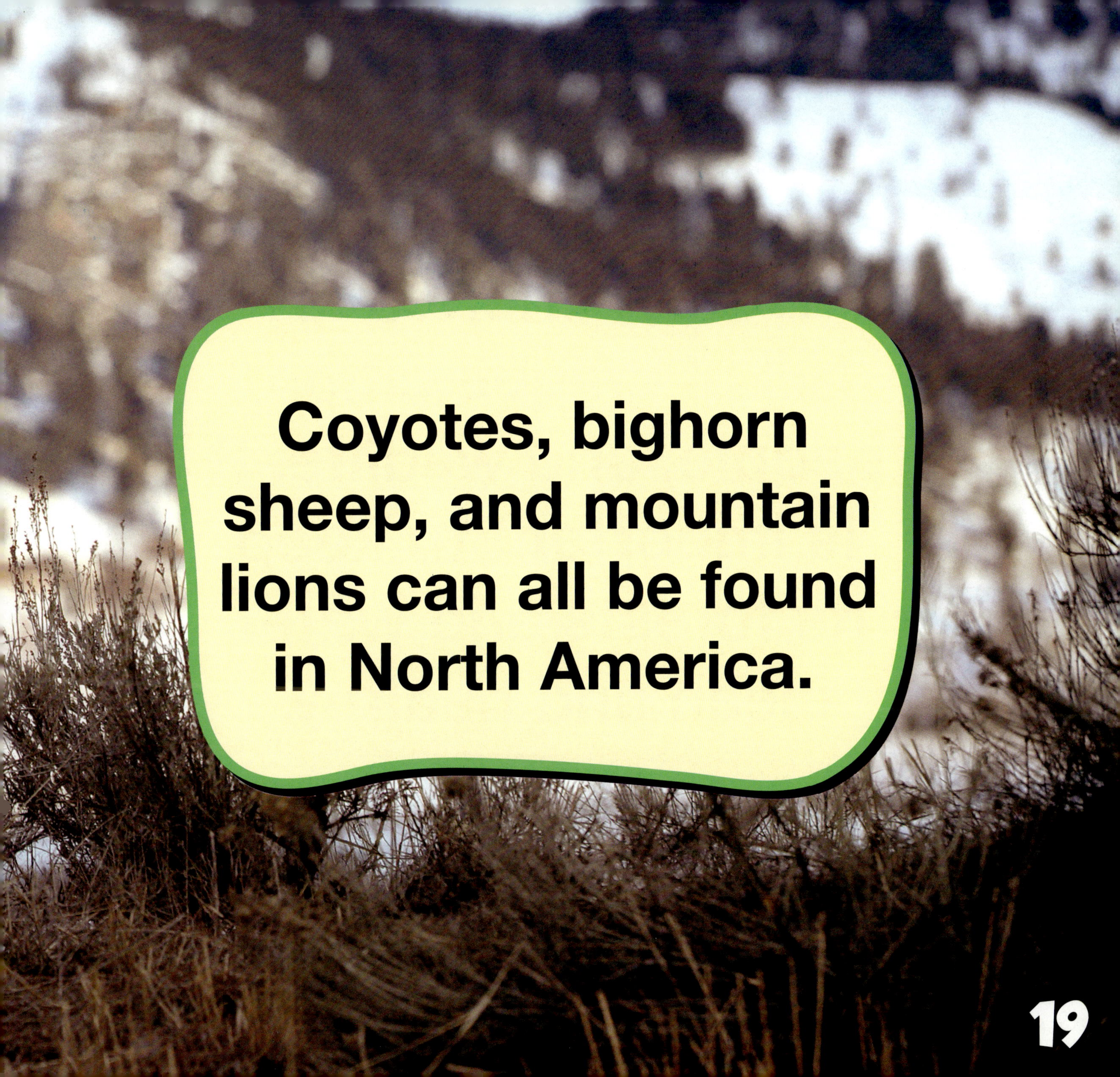

Coyotes, bighorn sheep, and mountain lions can all be found in North America.

North America is full of unique cities, people, and wildlife. It is important to keep its forests and water clean and healthy.

There are about **580 million** people living in **North America.**

Denali is the **tallest** mountain in **North America.** It is **20,310 feet** tall. (6,190 meters)

The **United States** has more than **250,000** rivers.

More than **8.1 million people** live in **New York City.** It is the **largest** city in the **United States.**

There are **31** states in **Mexico.**

There are **965** known **mammals** living in **North America.**

KEY WORDS

Research has shown that as much as 65 percent of all written material published in English is made up of 300 words. These 300 words cannot be taught using pictures or learned by sounding them out. They must be recognized by sight. This book contains 39 common sight words to help young readers improve their reading fluency and comprehension. This book also teaches young readers several important content words, such as proper nouns. These words are paired with pictures to aid in learning and improve understanding.

Page	Sight Words First Appearance
4	Earth, is, on, the
7	and, are, different, in, most, take, there, up
8	about, city, live, people
11	for, its, rivers
12	between, found, great, of, some, they
15	animals, land, many, plants
16	trees, world
19	all, be, can
20	important, it, keep, to, water

Page	Content Words First Appearance
4	continent, North America
7	Canada, countries, United States
8	Mexico City
11	forests, lakes, Missouri
15	bison
16	California, redwoods
19	bighorn sheep, coyotes, mountain lions
20	cities, people, water, wildlife

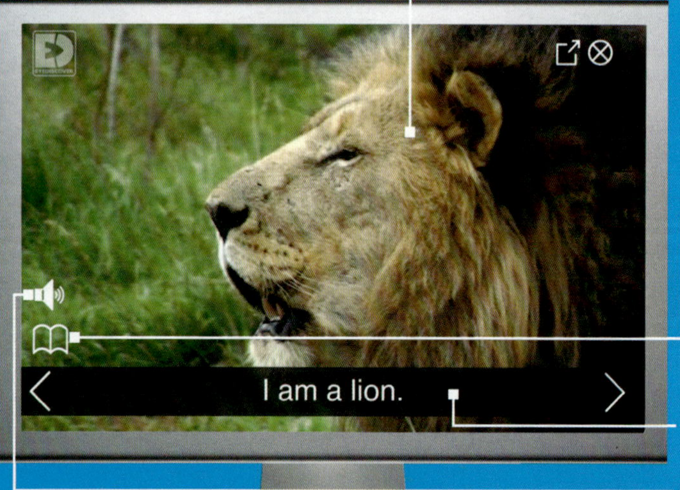

Watch
Video content brings each page to life.

Browse
Thumbnails make navigation simple.

Read
Follow along with text on the screen.

Listen
Hear each page read aloud.

Go to www.eyediscover.com and enter this book's unique code.

BOOK CODE

AVC33949